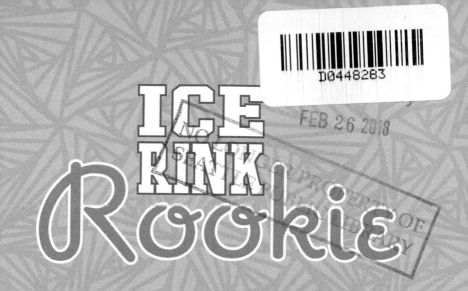

ICE RINK Rookie

BY JAKE MADDOX

text by Wendy L. Brandes
illustrated by Katie Wood

STONE ARCH BOOKS
a capstone imprint

Jake Maddox Girl Sports Stories are published by Stone Arch Books
a Capstone imprint
1710 Roe Crest Drive
North Mankato, Minnesota 56003
www.mycapstone.com

Library of Congress Cataloging-in-Publication Data
Names: Maddox, Jake, author.
Title: Ice rink rookie / by Jake Maddox ; text by Wendy L. Brandes ;
illustrated by Katie Wood.
Description: North Mankato, Minnesota : Stone Arch Books, a
Capstone imprint, [2018] | Series: Jake Maddox girls sports stories |
Summary: Pilar Ramirez loves to skate on ice, and normally she does
not keep being born without part of her right foot a secret, but when
her best friend convinces her to try out for the local hockey team, Pilar
decides not to mention her condition — but hockey presents her with
some problems that plain skating did not, and Pilar needs to learn
that being part of a team means being open with your teammates,
so that they understand all your strengths and weaknesses.

Identifiers: LCCN 2017038650 (print) | LCCN 2017039195 (ebook) |
ISBN 9781496558527 (eBook PDF) | ISBN 9781496558480 (hardcover) |
ISBN 9781496558503 (pbk.)

Subjects: LCSH: Hockey stories. | Children with disabilities—Juvenile
fiction. | Teamwork (Sports)—Juvenile fiction. | Best friends—Juvenile
fiction. | Friendship—Juvenile fiction. | CYAC: Hockey—Fiction. | People
with disabilities—Fiction. | Teamwork (Sports)—Fiction. | Best friends—
Fiction. | Friendship—Fiction. | Hispanic Americans—Fiction.

Classification: LCC PZ7.M25643 (ebook) | LCC PZ7.M25643 Ic 2018
(print) | DDC 813.6 [Fic] —dc23

LC record available at https://lccn.loc.gov/2017038650

Designer: Brent Slingsby
Production Specialist: Tori Abraham
Design Elements: Shutterstock: Essi

Printed and bound in Canada.
010805S18

TABLE OF CONTENTS

CHAPTER ONE

Join the Team!

Pilar Ramirez skated around the ice. Free skating time was almost over, but she wanted to do one last lap. She zipped around the final curve. She loved going fast!

As Pilar came off the ice, she saw her best friend waving to her. Her friend Sarah was wearing a hockey uniform. She was about to practice with her hockey team, the Frost Valley Ice Dogs.

"Hey, Pilar!" Sarah said, walking over. "I didn't know you were coming to the rink today."

"Hi! Yeah, my mom was supposed to be busy all afternoon, but her plans got canceled. So I asked her to bring me over," Pilar replied. "Skating is so much fun!"

"You know, I was watching you skate. With your kind of speed, you could be a great hockey player," Sarah said.

Pilar laughed. This wasn't the first time Sarah had mentioned hockey to her. "Are you trying to get me to join the Ice Dogs again?" she asked.

Sarah smiled. "Maybe! But seriously," she added, "it would be awesome to have you on the team. Just think about it. BFFs on the ice together!"

"It does sound pretty great," Pilar admitted. "And I have been thinking about trying a team sport. I don't know a lot about hockey, though."

"That doesn't matter," Sarah said. "Coach Grace is a great teacher. Plus, our team really needs more players. We have fourteen girls, but we need sixteen. If we don't get a full team, we can't play."

"I'll think about it," Pilar said. Then she paused. "But if I try out, you have to promise you won't tell anyone about my foot."

Usually, Pilar didn't hide the fact that she had been born without part of her right foot. But this time was different.

Sarah looked surprised. "Really?" she asked. "Why do you want to keep it a secret?"

"I don't want any special treatment," Pilar explained. "I wouldn't want anyone to act differently because they feel sorry for me."

"All right. I won't say anything," Sarah promised. "So, does that mean you'll come to our next practice and try out?"

Pilar thought for a second. She did like ice skating, and it would be fun to be on a team with her friend. Plus, she was always up for new challenges.

Finally, Pilar nodded. "I'm in! BFFs on ice!" she shouted.

CHAPTER TWO

The Ice Dogs

Two days later, Pilar's mom pulled up to the ice arena. Pilar was going to her first practice with the Frost Valley Ice Dogs.

Ms. Ramirez hugged Pilar. "Have fun today!" she said. "Just work hard like you always do. I'm sure you'll do great."

"Thanks, Mom!" Pilar said, stepping out of the car. Then she headed into the arena.

As soon as Pilar opened the door, Sarah rushed over. "I'm so glad you're here!" she said. "Are you ready to meet everyone?"

"Yeah, let's go!" Pilar replied, smiling.

Sarah led Pilar to an exercise room. A bunch of Ice Dogs were there stretching.

"Hey, everybody," Sarah said. "This is Pilar. She's practicing with us today."

In a blur, Pilar met Julia, Christina, Shea, Rachel, and Erika. "Hi!" Pilar said. "I don't know a lot about hockey, but I'm excited to learn."

"You'll figure things out!" Christina said.

"Definitely," Rachel added. "I didn't even know what icing was when I joined."

"You mean icing means something other than frosting on a cake?" Pilar asked.

All the girls laughed — except Julia.

"Wow, you really do have a lot to learn!" Julia said, crossing her arms.

Pilar glanced over at Sarah. She had a feeling Julia was going to be tougher on her than the other girls.

The team finished stretching and went to the locker room. Sarah gave Pilar a hockey sweater, pads, and a helmet. Then Pilar sat at the very end of the bench, away from the rest of the girls. She started changing into her new gear.

After she put on her thick hockey socks, Pilar pulled on her right skate. It had a special mold inside that allowed her to push off with her right foot. Pilar was glad she had some privacy. She didn't want the other girls to see her foot and feel sorry for her.

When they had changed, the girls went onto the ice. Pilar felt awkward in the hockey gear. Skating with so much padding was tricky.

As she took a turn, Pilar lost her balance and fell. She sat on the ice for a few seconds. Getting up was always hard because she couldn't push off as well with her right foot.

I need to work on getting up faster. I can't take this long in a game! Pilar thought.

As Pilar was getting to her feet, Coach Grace came onto the ice with another player. The girl, Avery, was also trying out for the team.

Coach Grace called everyone together. "I'm so excited to have Pilar and Avery trying out today!" she said. "I'd like to see how they skate with the team. So, let's do our regular warm-up and skate around the rink. Go!"

The girls raced down the ice. Pilar was toward the front of the pack. She felt really good about how fast she could skate.

After three laps, Coach Grace took Pilar and Avery aside. She asked them to skate backward. Pilar was able to do it easily, but slowly. Avery had been on a travel team before and went a lot faster than Pilar.

"Well, you're both great skaters," Coach said when they had finished. "I would love to have you two join the team!"

Pilar and Avery high-fived. The other girls skated over to congratulate them.

Sarah hugged Pilar. "I knew you could do it!" she exclaimed.

Coach Grace asked for quiet. "Now that we have a full team, we can really get going!" she said. "I want everyone to welcome Pilar and Avery to the team. Also, Pilar has never played hockey before, so I want you all to help her learn the rules."

Just then, Pilar heard Julia mumble, "That's sure not going to be easy."

Pilar laughed to herself. *I don't have to worry about* Julia *giving me any special treatment!*

* * *

After the girls finished warming up, Coach Grace asked everyone to get their sticks. Pilar skated up to the coach.

"Do you have a stick I could borrow for today, Coach?" Pilar asked.

"Of course," Coach Grace said, skating over to the boards. She handed Pilar a stick that came up to Pilar's eyes.

This is way too big! Pilar thought. It was hard to hold the stick and keep her balance while she skated.

Coach Grace set up cones on the ice with pucks next to them. For the drill, the girls would skate to the pucks and tap them with their sticks.

When it was Pilar's turn, she raced to the puck. But she had a hard time slowing down to tap it. She slid past the puck and reached back to get it. *Splat!* Down she went.

Sarah skated over. She offered Pilar a hand. "Don't worry. That's happened to all of us!" she said.

"You'll get the hang of it," Christina added.

I'm glad that Sarah helped me up. If she hadn't, it might have taken me a while, Pilar thought as she rejoined the group. *I'm just going to have to work twice as hard to become a good player.*

CHAPTER THREE

Practice, Practice, Practice

"Wow, Pilar, you look so much better with your stick!" Sarah said a few days later during practice. The girls had just finished the puck-tapping drill. This time, Pilar did it smoothly. And without falling.

"Thanks! Everything is easier now that I have my own stick. It's actually the right size," Pilar said as they skated around the rink. "I still need to work on getting up after a fall, though. I'm way too slow."

"But that's only because of your foot," Sarah pointed out. "Maybe you should say something to Coach. She might be able to give you some advice."

"No way! Like I told you before, I don't want any special treatment," Pilar replied.

Suddenly Julia zipped by. "Pick up the pace! This isn't free skating time!" she shouted.

Pilar watched Julia speed around the rink. "Is she always so bossy?" Pilar asked her friend.

"Julia can be super intense," Sarah admitted. "She really wants us all to get better and to win."

"I guess there's nothing wrong with that. Except if she isn't nice about it," Pilar said.

Coach Grace blew her whistle. The team gathered around her. "Today, we'll be doing a scrimmage. It'll be fun, and you'll all get some ice time in a gamelike setting."

Pilar was excited to see how it would feel to be in a game. *I know I'm not quite ready, but I'll give it my best shot!* she thought.

Coach Grace divided the girls into two teams. Pilar, Sarah, Julia, and Christina were the defense on Pilar's team. The girls had taught Pilar that the defense worked in pairs. Their job was to keep the puck away from their team's goal. The offense had lines made of three girls, and they tried to score.

Pilar had also learned that everyone gets super tired in hockey. So players on the bench replaced girls on the ice. On defense, that switch happened when your team had the puck in the other team's zone.

In the first shift, Coach Grace paired Pilar and Sarah together. Pilar was happy to be on the ice with her friend.

During their turn, Pilar made a few mistakes. But it wasn't all bad. She was getting a better feel for the flow of the game.

"Phew! That was really tiring," Pilar told Sarah as they came off the ice. "My legs feel like jelly!"

Sarah laughed. "You'll get used to it. You did a good job out there!"

Pilar smiled too. She was glad her best friend was so supportive.

After a few more minutes, Coach Grace blew her whistle. "Take a break and get some water, girls," she said. "Then we'll continue the scrimmage with new lines and defensive pairings."

While the girls were getting water, Julia came up to Pilar. "Hey, I was watching you when you were playing," she said. "I know you're new, but you have to be more careful when you handle the puck. It was sloppy, and mistakes add up in a real game."

Pilar had figured Julia would be extra tough on her. "Thanks for the pointer," she replied.

As Julia walked away, Pilar thought more about what she had said. *I hope I'll be able to remember everything during a real game!*

CHAPTER FOUR

Game On

"I can't believe our first game is already here!" Pilar exclaimed. She and Sarah were walking into the ice arena.

"I know!" Sarah agreed. "It was just two weeks ago that you joined the Ice Dogs."

"I'm so nervous. Are the Eels a really good team?" Pilar asked. The girls pushed through the locker room door.

"They're pretty good," Sarah replied. "It should be a tough game."

"I hope I don't forget the rules," Pilar whispered.

"You won't. And even if you do, everyone makes mistakes," Sarah said.

"But I'm still having a hard time getting up after I fall. What if I mess things up for the team?" Pilar asked.

Sarah put her arm around her friend's shoulder. "Don't worry so much. We win or lose as a team," she said. "It's not one person's responsibility."

Almost all the girls had arrived already. They were in the exercise room, getting loose. So Pilar and Sarah quickly changed and joined them.

When they went in, music was playing. Some of the girls were jumping around.

Christina bounced over. "Pilar! Sarah!" she yelled. "Are you excited for the game?"

"Ice Dogs! Ice Dogs!" Erika shouted.

Pilar laughed. "You guys have gone nuts!"

Julia clapped her hands. "We need to be on the ice for warm-up in five minutes."

The girls hit the ice. Music blasted from the arena speakers as they skated. People were starting to fill the stands.

Pilar loved the energy in the rink. She could feel her nerves starting to disappear.

As they finished their warm-up, Coach Grace called the team together. "You girls are ready for this game," she said. "I want you to have fun, play smart, and listen to your teammates. Now, let's go over the pairings and lineups for today."

The girls listened as the coach went through her list. "Pilar and Julia, you'll be together," Coach Grace announced.

I wish she had put me with Sarah, Pilar thought. *I'm going to be extra nervous with Julia. I hope I don't make any big mistakes!*

* * *

Pilar and Julia would be the third defensive team on the ice. Watching from the bench, Pilar cheered as the Ice Dogs started off strong. The offense had three shots on goal in the first few minutes.

When Pilar went onto the ice for the first time, her heart was beating fast. But then she saw her mom waving from the stands. It calmed her down right away.

Just do your best, she reminded herself. *And have fun.*

Rachel, Shea, and Avery were on offense. They moved the puck over the blue line into the Eels' zone. Pilar and Julia followed behind.

Avery passed to Pilar. Feeling nervous, Pilar quickly flicked the puck to Julia.

Julia took it and started to move, but two Eels came after her. She skated around them and passed back to Pilar.

A different Eels player rushed toward Pilar. Without thinking, Pilar dodged the Eel. She slapped the puck to Avery.

Moving closer to the net, Avery acted like she was going to shoot. At the last second, she passed to Rachel.

The Eels' goalie didn't notice Rachel, who was on the other side of the goal. Rachel blasted the puck into the net.

Score! The Ice Dogs took the lead, 1–0.

Pilar jumped up and down. She had been part of a scoring play! The girls gathered together for a group hug.

"Your shot was so awesome, Rachel!" Pilar said.

"Avery's pass was amazing!" Rachel replied.

"And Pilar and Julia did a great job of keeping the puck away from the Eels. It gave us time to set up!" Shea added.

The girls skated to the bench and high-fived the rest of their teammates. Pilar sat down, grinning. She was feeling good. *I love this team!* she thought.

CHAPTER FIVE

Slipping Up

Pilar glanced at the scoreboard. It was already the second period, and the Ice Dogs still had their 1–0 lead. The defense was playing great. The Eels had only five shots on goal.

With four minutes left in the second period, Pilar felt more confident as she took the ice. She was skating well, and she was controlling the puck. She had made hardly any newbie mistakes.

Right after Pilar started her shift, the Eels stole the puck. An Eel rushed over to the Ice Dogs' goal. Pilar reached out with her stick. She poked the puck away from the other player. It slid down the boards.

Shea took the puck and skated toward the Eels' net. Pilar followed. But since she was a defensive player, she wasn't sure how far forward she should go.

If I stay too far back, I might not be able to help the offense, Pilar thought. So, she crept in closer to the Eels' net.

Shea slapped the puck over to Avery. She skated around the net and took a shot.

The Eels' goalie blocked it, and the puck bounced away. Shea got her stick on it again. She sent it toward the back of the zone.

But as the puck came flying down the ice, Pilar realized she had skated too far forward. She wasn't in the right spot to get the puck. It slid right by her.

Pilar felt terrible. She had just made her first big rookie mistake.

An Eels' winger zoomed by and took the puck. Julia raced to catch up, but the Eel was too far ahead. The winger faked to her right, and then took a shot at the Ice Dogs' goal. The puck hit the back of the net.

The goal buzzer blared. It was now 1–1.

Julia and Pilar went back to the bench, catching their breath. *I'm the reason they got the breakaway,* Pilar thought. *I'm the reason they scored.*

"I know I shouldn't have gone so far into the zone," Pilar mumbled.

Julia heard her. "You need to think more about what you're doing!" she snapped.

Pilar looked down at her skates. She didn't expect Julia to be supportive, but her teammate made her feel worse.

At the end of the second period, the score was still tied. *I hope my mistake doesn't cost us the game,* Pilar thought. *I have to be even more careful during the third period.*

* * *

With two minutes left in the game, the teams were still tied. Sarah and Christina were out on defense. Julia and Pilar would be the next defensive pair to go on the ice.

Pilar didn't want to be playing during such an important situation. But she knew Sarah and Christina were getting tired. They would have to come off soon.

Plus, Julia is our team's best defender. We have to be out there, Pilar thought.

Sarah skated in, and Pilar hopped onto the ice. "Good luck, P!" Sarah shouted.

The Eels had the puck in the center of the rink. They were making a move to score. Pilar skated backward to protect the Ice Dogs' net.

One of the Eels spun around Julia and headed toward the goal. The Eel started to take her shot.

Pilar leaned forward and awkwardly poked at the puck. She lost her balance and landed on the ice with a *thump*. The puck slid right in front of the Ice Dogs' net.

Pilar struggled to her feet. She tried to get to the puck, but she wasn't fast enough. The Eels' center rushed forward. She brought her stick up and slammed the puck.

Before Pilar could blink, the puck was in the back of the net. Pilar's heart sunk. *They scored again because of me!* she thought.

Thirty seconds later, the game was over. It was a 2–1 Coldwater Eels win.

Julia quickly skated past Pilar and off the ice. Pilar knew that Julia was angry at Pilar's two big mistakes. But as mad as Julia might be, Pilar was even more upset with herself.

CHAPTER SIX

Teammate Troubles

Pilar and the rest of the team followed Coach Grace into the locker room. The coach gathered everyone together.

"Ice Dogs! I know you're disappointed we didn't win, but it was a great game," Coach Grace said. "Everyone worked as a team. I'm so proud of all of you! I'll see you back here for practice tomorrow."

Most of the girls started taking off their skates. As Pilar was putting away her equipment, Julia sat down next to her.

"I know you're upset about the game, so maybe this isn't the best time to talk," Julia began. "But you made some big mistakes."

Pilar felt like she was going to cry. "I know. I have a lot to learn," she said. "I'm trying my best."

"I know you're trying. But you have to learn how far forward you can skate in when the team is on offense," Julia said. "Plus, you have to get up more quickly after you fall!"

Pilar didn't say anything. She just sniffed, holding back tears.

"Listen, I wouldn't be a good teammate if I didn't call you out when you're having issues, Pilar," Julia continued. "Your rookie mistakes could hold the team back."

Christina, Shea, and Sarah overheard Julia. They all got into the conversation.

"Julia, you don't have to make Pilar feel bad," Christina said.

"Yeah," Shea added. "We lost as a team. It wasn't all her fault."

Sarah walked over to Julia. "Plus, you have no idea how hard some skills are for her! Pilar was born with only part of her right foot," Sarah blurted out. "She's working so hard. You need to back off."

The other girls looked surprised. They stared at Pilar. She felt her cheeks get hot. She couldn't believe that her best friend had just told her secret.

"I have never blamed my foot for anything," Pilar said quickly. She tried to stay calm. "Listen, Julia, if you want to call me out, that's fine. But you can do it in a nicer way."

Before Julia could say anything, Pilar got up and walked to the exercise room.

Maybe this hockey thing isn't going to work out after all, Pilar thought. She was angry with Julia for being so tough, with Sarah for telling her secret, and with herself for not being a good enough player.

CHAPTER SEVEN

Quitting?

Pilar sat on a bench in the exercise room. She couldn't stop thinking about her mistakes during the game. They had caused the team to lose.

Sarah came in and sat next to her friend. "I'm so sorry I told everyone about your foot," she whispered.

"I told you not to say anything," Pilar said, still upset.

"I know," Sarah replied. "I just couldn't keep quiet. Julia was being so hard on you. It wasn't fair."

"She's hard on everyone. I don't want anyone to think of my foot as an excuse," Pilar said.

"Nobody would think that," Sarah argued. "You're working so hard."

Pilar didn't say anything. She was working really hard, but it didn't seem to be enough.

"Well, no matter what, I'll have your back," Sarah said. "In fact, all the other girls have your back too. We're a team."

"Thanks. But after today's game, I feel like I might not be cut out for hockey," Pilar admitted.

"That's silly. I know my BFF doesn't have any quit in her!" Sarah exclaimed.

Pilar tried to smile. But all she could think was that maybe the team would be better off without her.

* * *

When Pilar had finished gathering her things, she went into the arena lobby. Pilar's mom was waiting for her.

Ms. Ramirez wrapped Pilar in a big hug. "You were terrific out there," she said.

Pilar sighed. "I'm not so sure. I think I might quit the team."

"Why, Pilar?" Ms. Ramirez asked, shocked. "You did a good job today."

"I made two big mistakes that cost us the game, Mom," Pilar said.

"You're new to hockey," Ms. Ramirez reminded her. "It's natural to make some mistakes. But you'll continue to improve."

Pilar shrugged. "There's a lot to learn. Maybe too much," she said. "Plus, I don't like feeling like I let the team down."

"You've never quit anything, Pilar. When things get tough, I can always count on you to get tougher," Ms. Ramirez said.

Pilar thought for a second. "I guess if I quit," she said slowly, "the Ice Dogs wouldn't have enough players. That would be letting the team down even more."

"That's true," her mom said.

"Maybe it wouldn't be so bad asking Coach for extra advice. And I could ask the girls for help too," Pilar added. "It could help me become a better player."

Ms. Ramirez hugged her again. "Exactly! You're part of a team. You don't have to work so hard all by yourself."

Before they had even left the rink, Pilar took out her cell phone. She texted Sarah and Christina, asking if they'd want to do some extra workouts with her.

CHAPTER EIGHT

Extra Ice Time

After the next team practice, Pilar asked Coach Grace for advice on getting up after a fall. At first, Pilar felt a little embarrassed. But the coach was happy to show her drills to try.

So throughout the week, Pilar met with Sarah and Christina at the rink before every Ice Dogs' practice. Together, they ran Coach's drills. The more Pilar practiced, the quicker she was able to get to her feet.

The girls also went over other hockey skills and strategies. Soon, Pilar knew exactly how far to skate in when the Ice Dogs were on offense.

Today was their last extra practice before their next game. Pilar felt good as they warmed up.

"Thanks for helping me," Pilar told her friends. "It's been so useful. I should've asked sooner!"

"I think all three of us have gotten better this week," Sarah added.

"Definitely," Christina said. "These practices were a great idea."

The ice rink was pretty crowded, so the girls set up cones near the end boards. They were working on passing. Suddenly, they heard someone call to them.

It was Julia. She skated over.

Pilar looked down at the ice. Julia and she had hardly talked since their last game.

"What are you three up to?" Julia asked.

"We've been doing some extra practice," Pilar explained. "Christina and Sarah have been helping me with my defense."

Julia looked surprised. "Really? That's great," she said. "I came to get in more ice time too. Can I skate with you guys?"

"Sure!" Christina replied.

Pilar worried that Julia might be bossy during their practice, but she was actually really nice and helpful. They exchanged some tips about positioning on defense. At one point, Julia showed Pilar a better way to hold her stick when shooting.

When they took a break, Julia skated over to Pilar. "Hey, I just wanted to say . . ." She took a breath. "I'm sorry for getting carried away after our last game. I want to be a good teammate, but sometimes I'm too intense."

"Thanks for apologizing," Pilar said. "That means a lot."

"It's impressive that you've been doing so much extra work," Julia added. Then she grinned. "It was worth it. You don't look like such a newbie anymore."

Pilar smiled too. "Thanks. I know you would only say that if you meant it."

"So, are you feeling ready to take on the Polar Bears at our next game?" Julia asked.

Pilar nodded. "If we all work together," she said, "I know we can win it!"

CHAPTER NINE

Another Chance

The second game of the season was against the Riverside Polar Bears. They were the Ice Dogs' biggest rival. It would be a tough game. But thanks to the extra practice, Pilar was feeling ready.

After the team warmed up, Coach Grace went over the lineups. Pilar was paired with Julia again on defense. This time, Pilar was happy to have her as a partner. *Being with Julia will only make me better,* she thought.

The Ice Dogs came out with a lot of energy. They kept pushing the puck into the offensive zone.

During Pilar and Julia's first shift, the Polar Bears grabbed the puck. They passed it forward. The puck sped toward the Ice Dogs' goal.

Pilar raced after the puck and got to it before the Polar Bears. She sent the puck to Shea.

"Nice speed!" Julia yelled.

Avery, Shea, and Erika took the puck closer to the Polar Bears' net. As they passed back and forth, Pilar and Julia skated up.

I need to be careful not to repeat my mistake! Don't go too far forward, Pilar thought. She was going to make sure the Polar Bears wouldn't start a breakaway.

The Ice Dogs kept moving the puck around. But a Polar Bear got her stick in to stop a pass.

Before the other player could even take a step, Pilar had raced over. She pushed the puck toward the boards. Pilar chased after it and slapped it forward to Avery.

Avery quickly passed to Shea. Then Shea blasted the puck at the net, but the Polar Bears' goalie caught it in her glove. No goal.

Pilar and Julia skated to the bench. Sarah and Christina took their place.

"Rats! That was a great scoring chance!" Pilar exclaimed, breathing heavily.

"I know," Julia said. "We almost took the lead. Great positioning and passing, though!"

Pilar grinned. "Thanks!" she said.

Through the first period, neither team scored. It was still 0–0 when Pilar and Julia went out in the second period.

The Polar Bears were attacking. A player took a shot from the back of the zone.

Pilar didn't hesitate. She dropped to the ice and blocked it. The puck bounced away. Pilar quickly got to her feet. She didn't even have time to feel good about getting up so fast. She zoomed after the puck and passed it to Avery.

Avery started to skate away from the Ice Dogs' goal, but a Polar Bear stole the puck. She took a hard shot. It hit the goal post and bounced back.

The Polar Bears' center skated after the puck. *Not so fast!* Pilar thought. She got to the puck first and sent it back to her team's offense.

Rachel picked up the pass. She headed toward the other side of the rink.

Phew! We're safe for now, thought Pilar as she and Julia skated off the ice.

When they sat on the bench, Julia grinned. "That was another great shift. Nice job keeping the puck away from the goal," she said.

So far so good, Pilar thought. *But we're getting so close to the end of the game. Every play is even more important now!*

CHAPTER TEN

Final Score

In the third period, the score was still tied 0–0. Both teams were pressing hard and moving fast.

With one minute left, Pilar and Julia got into the action. *This is it. Our last chance to score,* Pilar thought.

The Polar Bears were attacking again. Their three forwards fanned out in front of the Ice Dogs' goal. A Polar Bear sent the puck spinning around the boards.

Pilar went low to dig the puck out of the corner. As she reached for it, she fell. She quickly scrambled to her feet and slapped the puck to Rachel.

But a Polar Bear wrestled it away from her. The Polar Bears brought the puck close to the Ice Dogs' goal. One of the defensive players took a shot.

The puck flew toward Pilar. She stopped it with her stick. As Pilar looked around, she realized something. A Polar Bears' defensive player had come really far forward.

She's skated in way too far. That's what I did in the last game. Here's our opportunity for a breakaway! Pilar thought.

With ten seconds left, Pilar smacked the puck over to Shea. The pass was near perfect. It hit Shea's stick right on the tape.

Six seconds left. Shea raced out of the zone. None of the Polar Bears could catch up to her. She went straight to the other team's goal. She slapped the puck.

The goalie had no chance. The puck flew into the right corner of the net. Score!

Just then the buzzer sounded. Time had run out. The Ice Dogs won, 1–0!

The girls on the ice jumped up and down. Pilar hugged all of her teammates. *We did it!* she thought. *It's so awesome to be a part of a real team win. Everybody helped!*

After the game, the Ice Dogs celebrated in the locker room. Sarah cranked up some music. The girls danced and cheered.

Sarah gave Pilar a huge hug. "Aren't you glad you decided to stay with the team?" she asked.

"For sure!" Pilar shouted over the music. "Being an Ice Dog is the best."

Julia danced over to Pilar. "You know, you saved the game. Twice!" she exclaimed. "You've really improved."

"Thanks, but I couldn't have done it alone," Pilar said. "Sarah and Christina helped me so much. And you did too, Julia."

"Just to warn you, though, I'm going to keep calling you out. That's what I think a good teammate does," Julia said.

"Good. I wouldn't want you going easy on me!" Pilar replied.

"But you've totally proved how tough you are," Julia added. "Congrats on a great game, rookie."

Pilar laughed. "I can't wait for our next one!"

Author Bio

Wendy L. Brandes writes books for children, including Capstone's Summer Camp series. Although she's never been able to skate a complete lap around a rink without falling, she's an avid hockey fan. She's even named a number of characters after players from her favorite team, the New York Rangers.

Illustrator Bio

Katie Wood fell in love with drawing when she was very small. Since graduating from Loughborough University School of Art and Design in 2004, she has been living her dream working as a freelance illustrator. From her studio in Leicester, England, she creates bright and lively illustrations for books and magazines all over the world.

Glossary

arena (uh-REE-nuh)—a large area that is used for sports or entertainment

drill (DRIL)—a repetitive exercise that helps you learn a specific skill

intense (in-TENS)—extreme or full of strong feelings

mold (MOLD)—an object that is made to fit exactly into or over a particular area

rookie (RUK-ee)—a person who is playing their first year on a team

scrimmage (SKRIM-ij)—a practice game

strategy (STRAT-uh-jee)—a careful plan for doing something

supportive (suh-PAWR-tiv)—giving help and encouragement

treatment (TREET-muhnt)—how others act or behave toward a person

Discussion Questions

1. Pilar is a hockey rookie. Talk about a time when you were new to a sport or an activity. How did you feel? How did you learn the new skills and routines?

2. In your own words, summarize why Pilar wanted to keep her foot a secret. What do you think about her decision? What would you have done?

3. Do you think Julia was being mean to Pilar, or was she just trying to help? Use examples from the story to support your answer. Was there anything Julia could have done differently?

Writing Prompts

1. What do you think makes a good teammate? Make a list of four things a good teammate does and four things she doesn't do.

2. Pilar learns that it's okay to ask her coach and teammates for help. Write two paragraphs about a time when you asked for help. How did it feel? Did asking for help make things easier or harder?

3. Rewrite the end of Chapter Five from Julia's point of view. Be sure to show what Julia is thinking and feeling.

Hockey Terms

Become an ice rink pro and check out some common hockey terms!

BOARDS — the wall surrounding the rink that keeps the puck in play

BREAKAWAY — when a player has the puck and there are no defensive players around to stop her from getting to the goal

DEFENSIVE PLAYERS — two players who play in front of their team's net and try to keep the other team from taking shots

LINE — the three offensive players that are on the ice at the same time. A line is made up of a center, a left wing, and a right wing. The wings (also called wingers) mostly play along the sides of the rink.

OFFENSIVE PLAYERS — players who play near the other team's net and try to score

PENALTY a punishment a player gets when she breaks a rule of the game. For example, if a player hits another player with her stick, a referee will send that player off the ice and into the penalty box. Depending on which rule was broken, the player can be in the box for two, four, five, or ten minutes.

SHIFT — the period of time that a line or a defensive pairing is on the ice

ZONE — one of the areas on the rink. Two blue lines divide the rink into three zones: the offensive zone, neutral zone, and defensive zone.

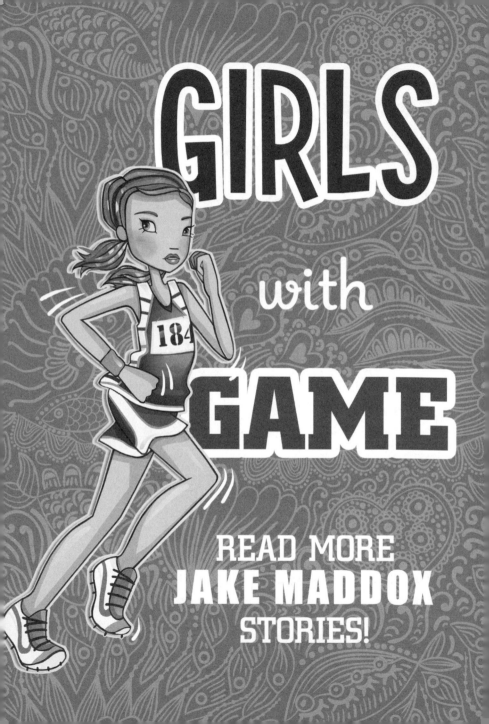

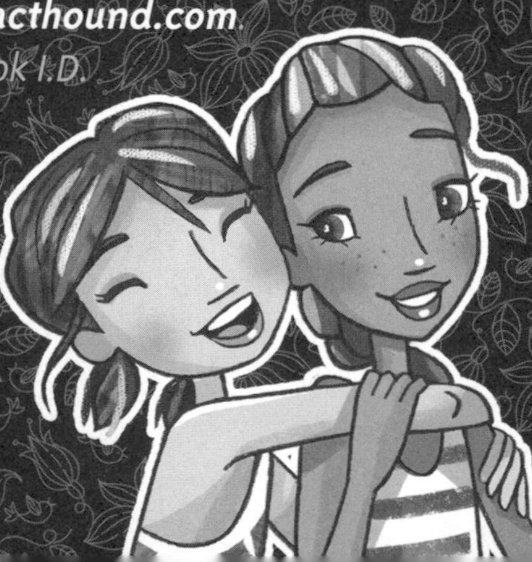